In the Darkness of the Night

NYX EVERNIGHT

Impressum:
Bibliografische Information der Deutschen Nationalbibliothek. Die
Deutsche Nationalbibliothek verzeichnet diese Publikation in der
Deutschen Nationalbibliografie; detaillierte bibliografische Daten
sind im Internet über http://dnb.d-nb.de abrufbar.
Veröffentlicht bei Infinity Gaze Studios AB
1. Auflage
September 2024
Alle Rechte vorbehalten
Copyright © 2024 Infinity Gaze Studios
Texte: © Copyright by Nyx Evernight
Cover & Buchsatz: V.Valmont @valmontbooks
Das Werk ist urheberrechtlich geschützt. Jede Verwertung
außerhalb des Urheberrechtsgesetzes ist ohne Zustimmung von
Infinity Gaze Studios AB unzulässig und wird strafrechtlich verfolgt.
Infinity Gaze Studios AB
Södra Vägen 37
829 60 Gnarp
Schweden
www.infinitygaze.com

IN THE DARKNESS OF THE NIGHT

NYX EVERNIGHT

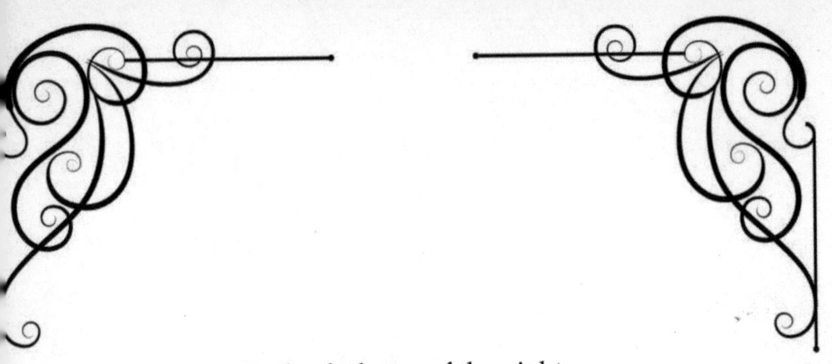

In the darkness of the night,
Shadows creep and haunt with fright,
Whispers echo through the air,
As something lurks without a care.

Fear takes hold and freezes bone,
As something wicked starts to roam,
Eerie silence, then a sound,
As something evil moves around.

Heart racing, panic sets in,
As something wicked seeks to win,
Closer now, it draws near,
As something wicked feeds on fear.

In the darkness of the night,
Shadows dance with pure delight,
And though we try with all our might,
Something wicked comes to light.

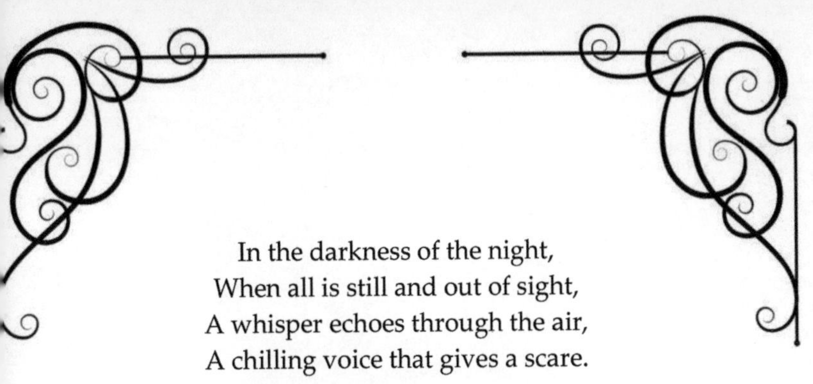

In the darkness of the night,
When all is still and out of sight,
A whisper echoes through the air,
A chilling voice that gives a scare.

The shadows dance upon the wall,
As eerie footsteps start to crawl,
A presence felt but never seen,
A terror like you've never been.

The hairs on your neck start to rise,
As fear takes hold and grips your thighs,
You try to run but cannot flee,
This nightmare is your destiny.

The moon is hidden behind the clouds,
As the haunting voice grows louder and proud,
The wind howls like a mournful beast,
As the terror of the night is released.

So be wary in the dark of night,
For evil lurks and takes delight,
In scaring those who dare to roam,
And turning your peaceful dreams to stone.

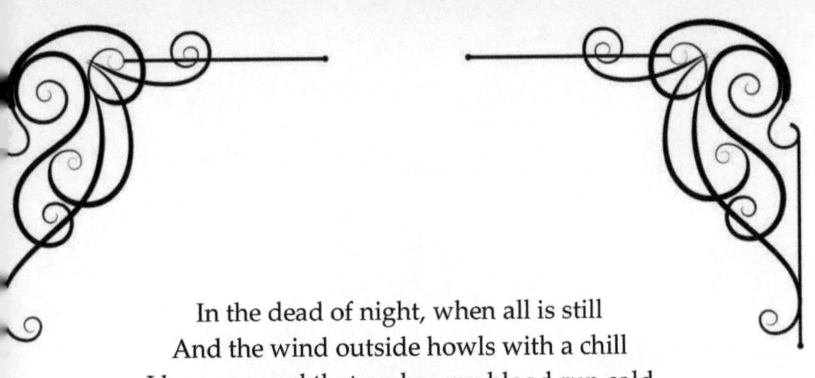

In the dead of night, when all is still
And the wind outside howls with a chill
I hear a sound that makes my blood run cold
A creaking, moaning, as if something old

Is stirring in the darkness,
coming for me I close my eyes
and try to flee
But there's nowhere to go,
nowhere to hide
From the thing that lurks just outside

Its breath is hot, its touch is cold
It whispers secrets that have never been told
And I know that if it catches me
I'll be lost for all eternity

So I run and run, until my legs give out
And I collapse, consumed by doubt
For I know that I can never escape
The horror that lies in wait.

In the darkness of the night,
As the moon rises high,
Whispers echo through the air,
And the shadows come alive.

They lurk in every corner,
And hide behind each door,
Watching with their beady eyes,
As you cross the creaky floor.

Their whispers turn to laughter,
As they follow you around,
Creeping closer ever slowly,
Until you hear their ghostly sound.

You try to run away from them,
But they're always one step ahead,
Chasing you down endless halls,
As you wish that you were dead.

For the shadows hold a secret,
A dark and eerie tale,
Of a world beyond the living,
Where the dead and ghosts prevail.

So beware the lurking shadows,
As you wander through the night,
For they're always watching, waiting,
To take you into their sight.

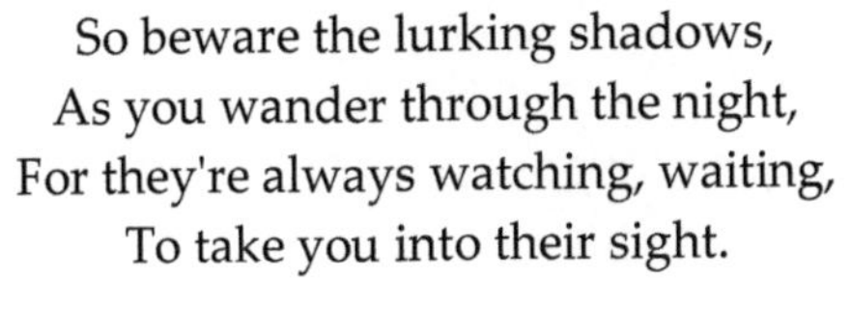

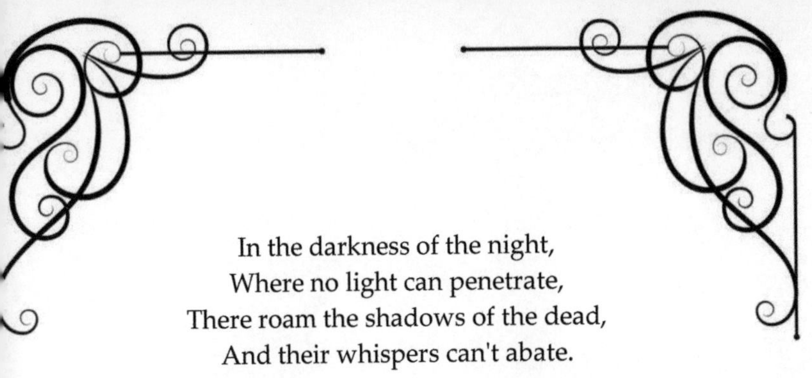

In the darkness of the night,
Where no light can penetrate,
There roam the shadows of the dead,
And their whispers can't abate.

They speak of things beyond our world,
Of creatures from the void,
And every sound that they make,
Fills the air with fear and dread.

The shadows crawl along the ground,
And climb up walls and trees,
And if you hear their voices,
You'll be brought down to your knees.

For they'll tell you of the horrors,
That lurk just out of sight,
And once they've filled your mind with fear,
They'll haunt you day and night.

So if you find yourself alone,
In the darkness of the night,
Beware the shadows that surround you,
And keep them out of sight.

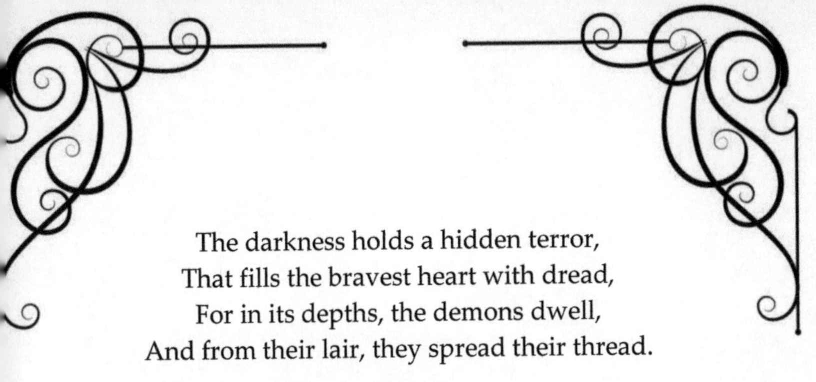

The darkness holds a hidden terror,
That fills the bravest heart with dread,
For in its depths, the demons dwell,
And from their lair, they spread their thread.

Their whispers echo through the void,
A warning to all who hear,
Of the horrors that await us all,
If we succumb to our fear.

They speak of ghastly apparitions,
Of ghosts that haunt the living,
And of the tortured souls who wander,
In search of peace and forgiving.

Their voices carry on the wind,
And fill the air with dread,
As they remind us of the darkness,
That hides within our head.

So if you find yourself alone,
In the darkness of the night,
Beware the demons lurking there,
And hold on to the light.

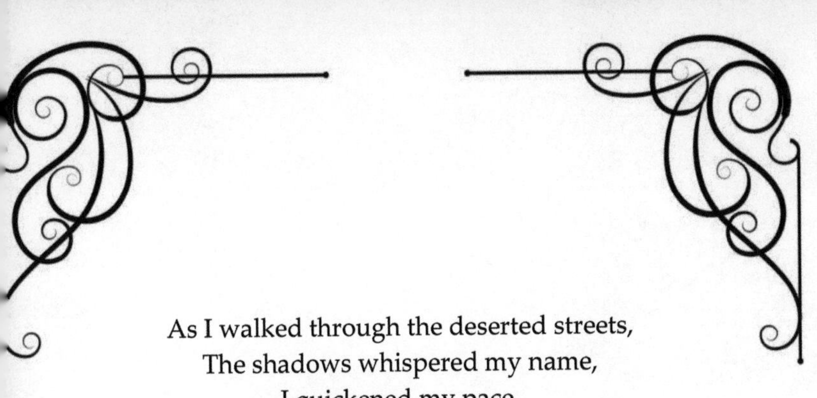

As I walked through the deserted streets,
The shadows whispered my name,
I quickened my pace,
but their voices grew louder,
And I felt my sanity wane.

I turned a corner and saw a figure,
Wrapped in a shroud of black,
Its eyes glowed like hot coals,
And I froze in my tracks.

The figure beckoned me closer,
And I felt a force pulling me near,
My heart pounded in my chest,
As I realized my greatest fear.

For in that moment, I knew,
That the shadows had taken me,
And I would never escape their grasp,
For all eternity.

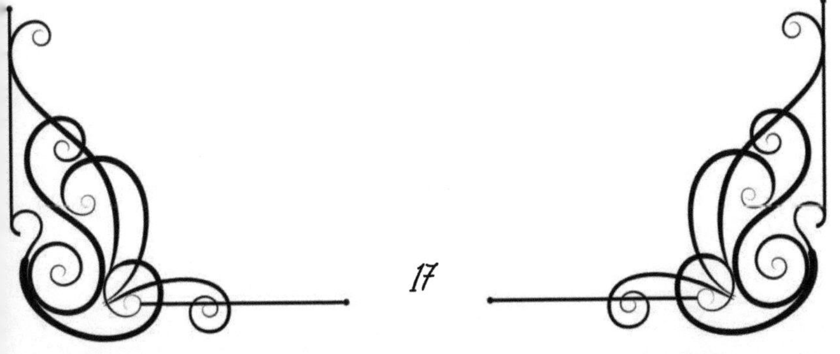

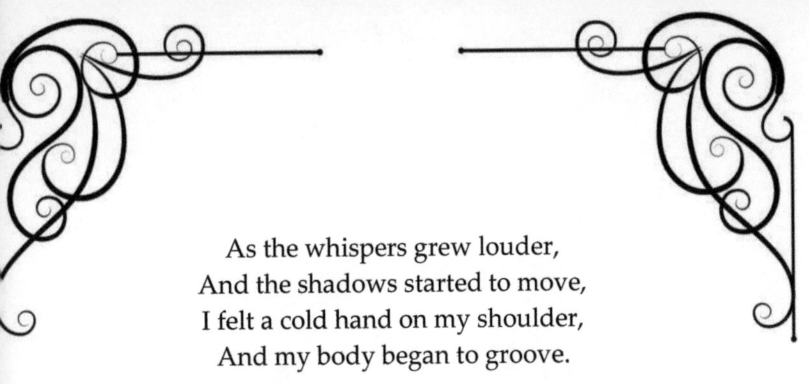

As the whispers grew louder,
And the shadows started to move,
I felt a cold hand on my shoulder,
And my body began to groove.

I couldn't control my own limbs,
As if possessed by some force,
The shadows danced around me,
And the whispers grew more coarse.

I screamed out for help,
But no one came to my aid,
I was trapped in this nightmare,
And the shadows had me waylaid.

Finally, as the sun began to rise,
The shadows slowly retreated,
Leaving me alone and shaken,
With a terror that could not be defeated.

From that day on, I lived in fear,
Of the darkness and the night,
For I knew that the shadows and their whispers,
Could return at any sight.

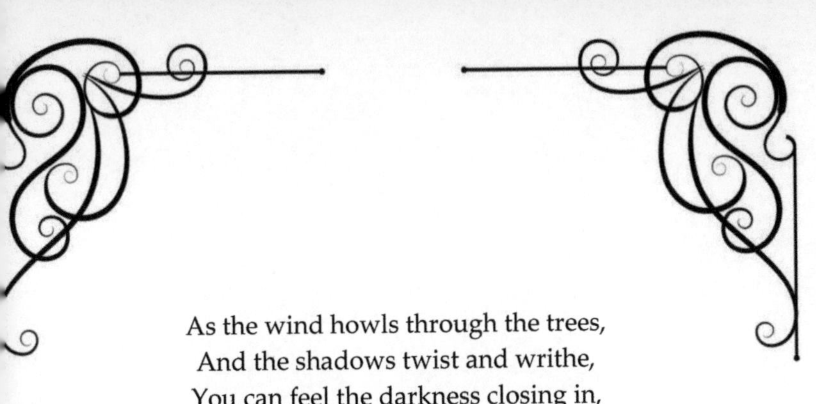

As the wind howls through the trees,
And the shadows twist and writhe,
You can feel the darkness closing in,
And the fear comes to life.

But if you can find the strength within,
To face the shadows and the night,
You may find that what once frightened you,
Is now your guiding light.

For in the depths of fear and dread,
There lies a power untold,
And those who brave the darkness,
May find that they have grown bold.

So let the shadows whisper,
Let the fear run wild and free,
For in facing our deepest terrors,
We may become who we were meant to be.

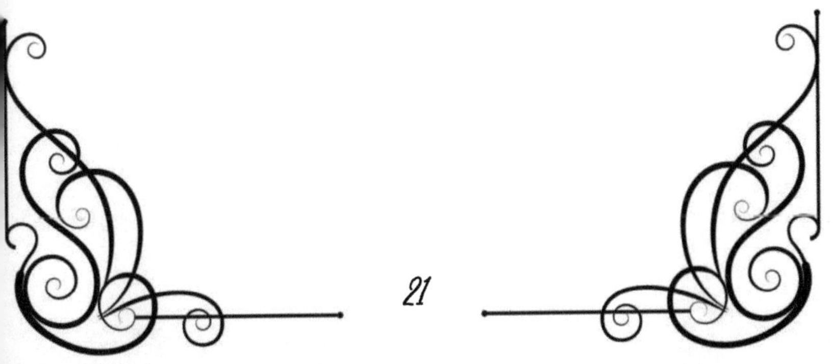

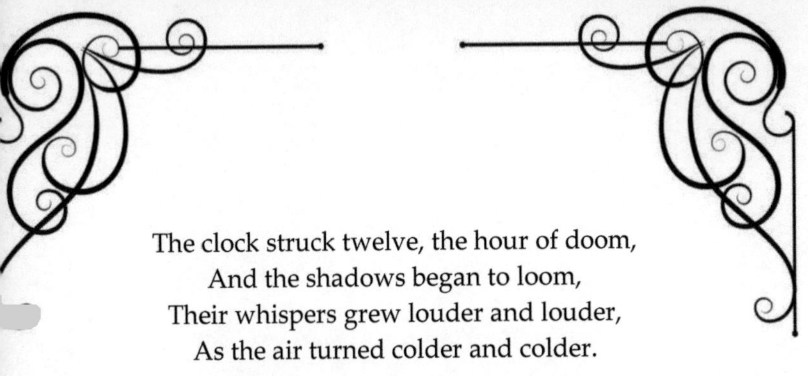

The clock struck twelve, the hour of doom,
And the shadows began to loom,
Their whispers grew louder and louder,
As the air turned colder and colder.

The darkness engulfed everything in sight,
And the shadows seemed to take flight,
Their forms shifting and changing,
As they danced in the moon's pale light.

The creatures of the void drew near,
Their eyes filled with an unearthly leer,
Their teeth sharp and their claws long,
As they sang their haunting song.

The shadows reached out with their hands,
And pulled me into their world of endless sands,
Where the dead danced and the living cried,
And the night sky was forever tied.

I tried to scream, but no sound would come,
As the shadows swallowed me whole and numb,
And now I roam this world of darkness and pain,
Forever bound to the shadows' dark reign.

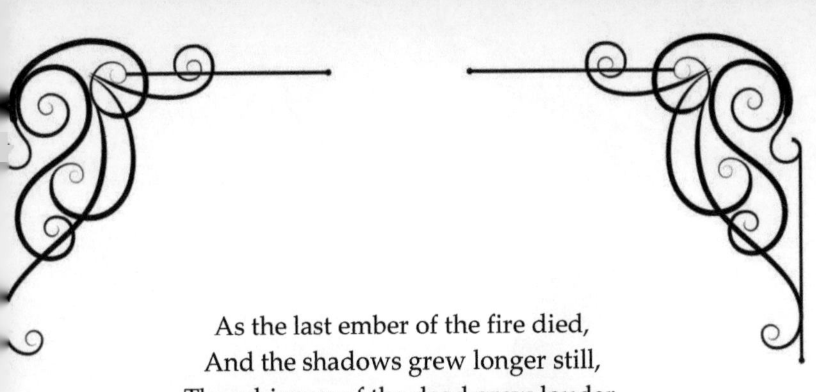

As the last ember of the fire died,
And the shadows grew longer still,
The whispers of the dead grew louder,
And the air grew cold and chill.

The boy could feel the hairs on his neck,
Stand up as the shadows closed in,
And he knew that he had to run,
Before the shadows claimed him.

He sprinted through the darkened streets,
With the shadows hot on his heels,
Their whispers echoing in his ears,
As he ran with all his might.

Finally, he reached the safety of home,
And bolted the door behind him tight,
But he knew that the shadows would come,
To haunt him throughout the night.

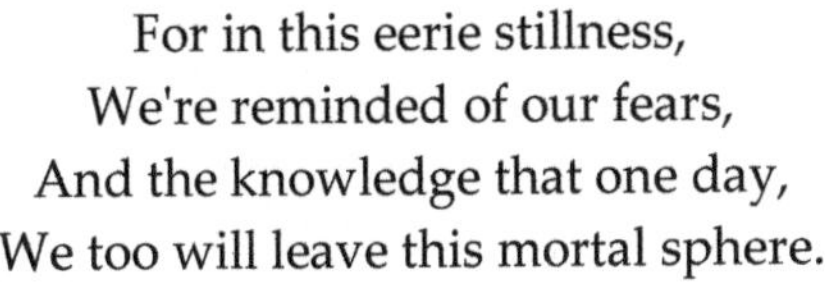

In the depths of the night,
The wind whispers a mournful song,
As the moon hangs low and bright,
And the shadows stretch out long.

The air is thick with sadness,
And the earth seems to weep,
For the ones who've left this world,
And their memories we must keep.

But amidst this melancholy,
There's a feeling of unease,
As though something wicked lurks,
And our fears it seeks to seize.

It's a chill that grips the heart,
And a shiver down the spine,
As we're haunted by the memories,
Of those who've passed beyond time.

So we stand there in the darkness,
Feeling lost and all alone,
As the wind sings a sad, creepy tune,
And the shadows claim their throne.

For in this eerie stillness,
We're reminded of our fears,
And the knowledge that one day,
We too will leave this mortal sphere.

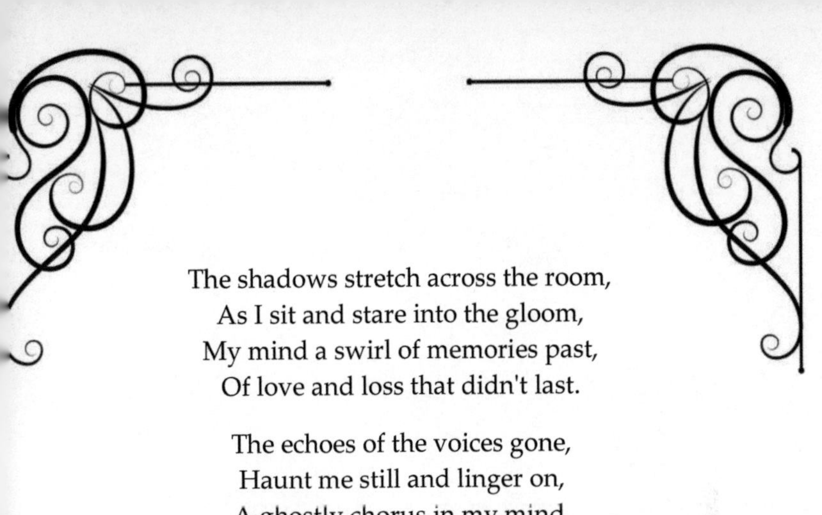

The shadows stretch across the room,
As I sit and stare into the gloom,
My mind a swirl of memories past,
Of love and loss that didn't last.

The echoes of the voices gone,
Haunt me still and linger on,
A ghostly chorus in my mind,
Of those who left me far behind.

I walk alone, a lonely soul,
With nothing but my thoughts to hold,
And though I try to leave behind,
The sadness that I cannot find.

It clings to me like cobweb strands,
A weight that I cannot withstand,
And in the darkness of my heart,
It tears me apart, bit by part.

So I sit and stare into the night,
As the shadows dance in the pale moonlight,
And I wonder if I'll ever find,
A way to leave the sadness behind.

A man alone, with sorrow in his heart,
Walks down a path, where shadows dart.
The leaves on the trees, they rustle and sway,
As if they're trying to lead him astray.

He walks through the woods, so dark and deep,
Where the trees grow close and the shadows creep.
The wind whispers softly, a mournful tune,
As if it's singing for those who've gone too soon.

The man he stops, and looks up to the sky,
Where the stars are shining, so bright up high.
But his eyes they fill, with tears and pain,
For the stars remind him, of one he'll never see again.

His footsteps falter, as he remembers the past,
The love he lost, and the memories that last.
The wind it picks up, and begins to howl,
As if it's mourning with the man's heart, so foul.

He continues on, with a heavy heart,
Feeling as if he's being torn apart.
The shadows they dance, and the wind it wails,
As if they're trying to tell him a tale.

A tale of love and loss, of pain and despair,
Of a man who lost everything, and was left to bear.
The weight of his sorrow, his burden to bear,
As he walks through the woods, in a state of despair.

The darkness grips my heart and soul,
A weight I cannot bear,
I wander through these empty halls,
With no one else to care.

The shadows dance along the walls,
And whisper in my ear, Telling tales of sorrow and
pain, Of all that I must fear.

My heart is heavy with regret,
For all that I have lost,
And every step I take feels like,
A never-ending cost.

The memories haunt me day and night,
Of all that I held dear,
And every moment feels like,
A journey filled with fear.

I try to find my way back home,
But everything's so cold,
The sadness and the darkness,
Have taken their firm hold.

And so I wander endlessly,
Through this sad and creepy place,
With nothing left to guide me,
But the tears upon my face.

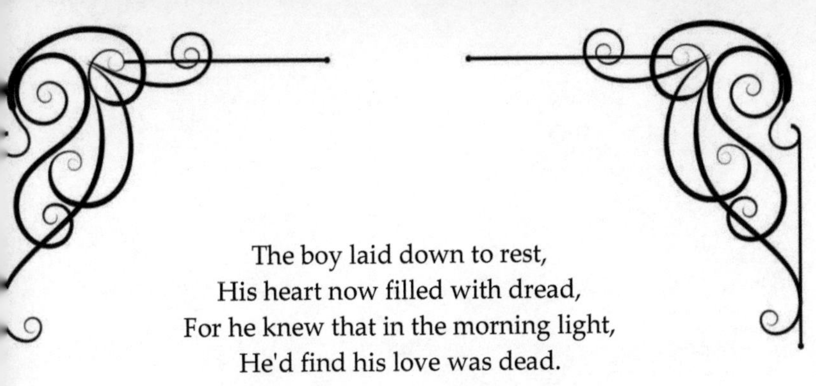

The boy laid down to rest,
His heart now filled with dread,
For he knew that in the morning light,
He'd find his love was dead.

And as he closed his eyes to sleep,
He heard a haunting sound,
The whisper of his lover's voice,
Echoing all around.

"I'll always be with you," she said, "
Even though I'm gone,
And though my body may be cold,
My love will linger on."

And so the boy wept bitter tears,
For the love he'd lost that day,
And the ghostly voice of his beloved,
Haunted him along the way.

For though she may have passed away,
Her spirit still remained,
A sad and creepy reminder,
Of the love that had been gained.

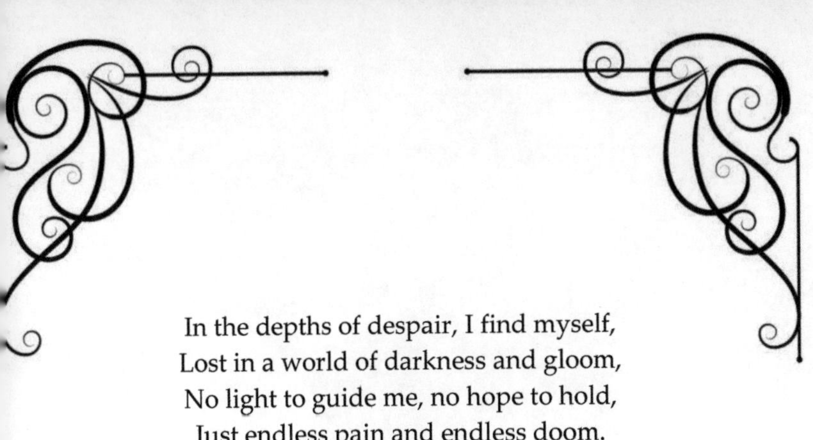

In the depths of despair, I find myself,
Lost in a world of darkness and gloom,
No light to guide me, no hope to hold,
Just endless pain and endless doom.

My heart is heavy with sorrow and grief,
As I trudge through the shadowy night,
Each step a struggle, each breath a burden,
As I try to make it to the light.

But the darkness surrounds me, a shroud of despair,
And I can't shake off the weight of my pain,
I'm trapped in this bleak, desolate world,
With nothing to lose and nothing to gain.

So I wander alone in the darkness,
A ghost in a world that's forgotten and dead,
And I know that I'll never find solace,
Just an endless abyss of sadness and dread.

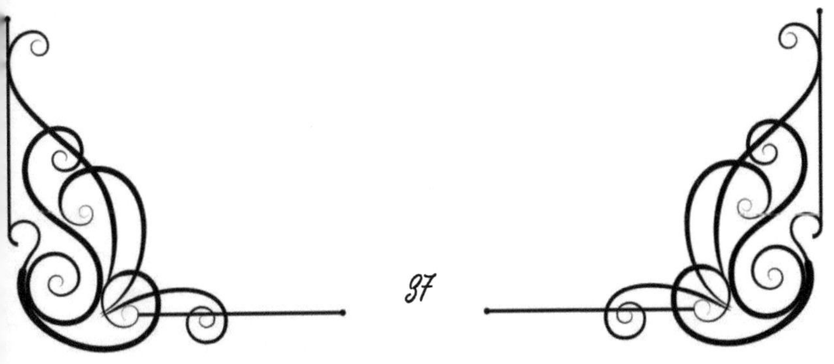

Darkness envelopes my soul,
As I wander through the night,
The weight of my sorrow dragging me down,
My heart consumed by blight.

The world is a bleak and empty place,
A vast and endless void,
My dreams and hopes have withered away,
And I'm left here, destroyed.

There is no joy, no light, no hope,
Just endless shades of gray,
And every day is a struggle,
Just to make it through the fray.

The darkness beckons me closer,
A siren call to the abyss,
And I'm torn between the pain of living,
And the sweet relief of eternal rest.

But I know I must keep going,
For the ones I've left behind,
Even though the weight of the darkness,
Threatens to crush my mind.

So I wander through the darkness,
Hoping to find a way, To lift the burden from my
soul, And find a brighter day.

Death, oh death, the great unknown,
The final journey we must take alone.
No one knows what lies ahead,
As we leave this world and join the dead.

Some say death is just a part of life,
A peaceful end to all our strife.
Others fear the darkness of the abyss,
And wonder if there's anything after this.

But whether we welcome it or fear it so,
Death is a fate we all must know.
Our time is fleeting, our days are few,
And death will come for me and you.

So let us live our lives with care,
And cherish every moment we have to spare.
For when our time on earth is through,
Death will come, and our journey anew.

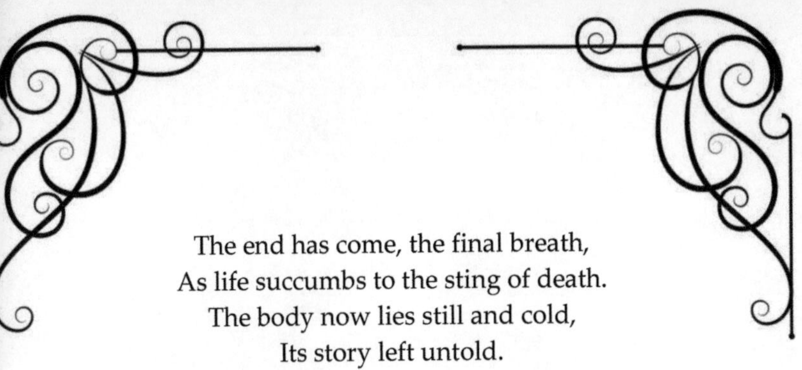

The end has come, the final breath,
As life succumbs to the sting of death.
The body now lies still and cold,
Its story left untold.

The spirit lingers, free to roam,
Through the veil to the unknown.
To find the answers we all seek,
In a place where time is weak.

Some say death is a door,
To a realm beyond our shore,
Where souls find eternal rest,
And all fears are laid to rest.

Others see it as a curse,
A punishment for a life's worth.
A bleak and endless void,
Where hopes and dreams are destroyed.

Yet in the end, it matters not,
Whether we believe or not.
For death is but a natural fate,
That we all must ultimately face.

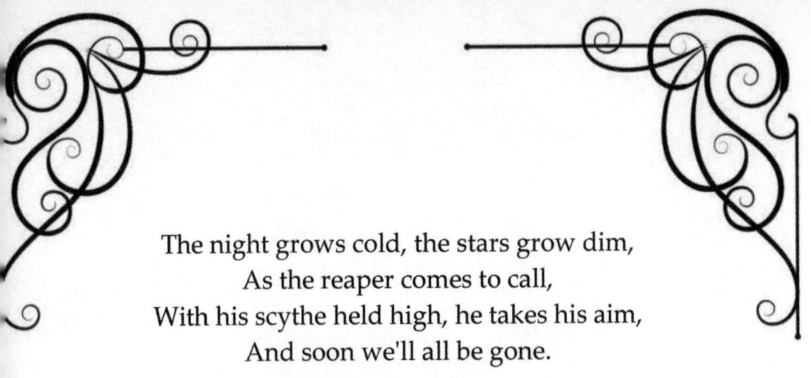

The night grows cold, the stars grow dim,
As the reaper comes to call,
With his scythe held high, he takes his aim,
And soon we'll all be gone.

He comes for rich and poor alike,
And for the young and old,
He takes us all without a care,
And leaves our bodies cold.

No one can escape his grasp,
Or bargain for more time,
For when our number's up, it's up,
And death is swift and final.

But though our bodies turn to dust,
And our spirits leave this earth,
Our memories will live on,
And keep our legacy in worth.

So fear not the reaper's call,
But live each day with care,
For when our time is up at last,
We'll leave behind our share.

The silence settles like a shroud,
As death steals its final breath,
And those left behind are left to grieve,
For the one who's met their death.

No more laughter, no more tears,
No more joys or fears,
For in death, all that's left behind,
Is a memory that slowly clears.

The body lies still and cold,
Lifeless and now at rest,
And those who loved them dearly,
Are left to mourn the loss, distressed.

But perhaps in death, there's solace,
A freedom from all pain,
And though we'll miss them dearly,
Perhaps they've found eternal gain.

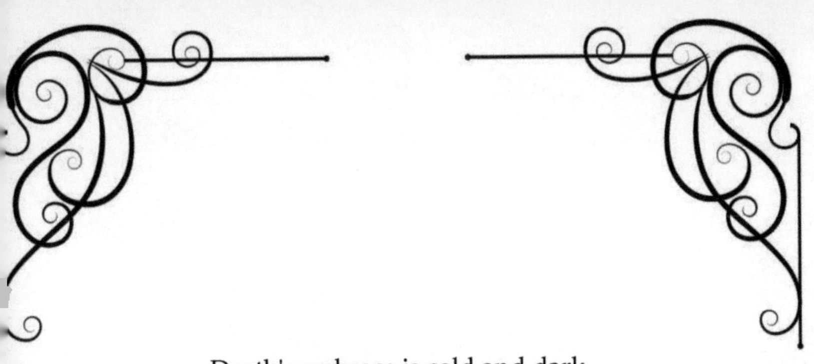

Death's embrace is cold and dark,
A final resting place for every heart.
It comes for us all, young and old,
Taking us to where mysteries unfold.

In Death's realm, time has no hold,
No more pain, no more stories untold.
All that's left is an endless sleep,
While loved ones on
Earth mourn and weep.

But perhaps Death is not so cruel,
For those who've suffered and been through hell.
It may be a relief, a final release,
A chance to escape life's endless disease.

So when Death comes knocking at my door,
I'll greet it with open arms and so much more.
For it is the end of life's great race,
And the start of a new and unknown place.

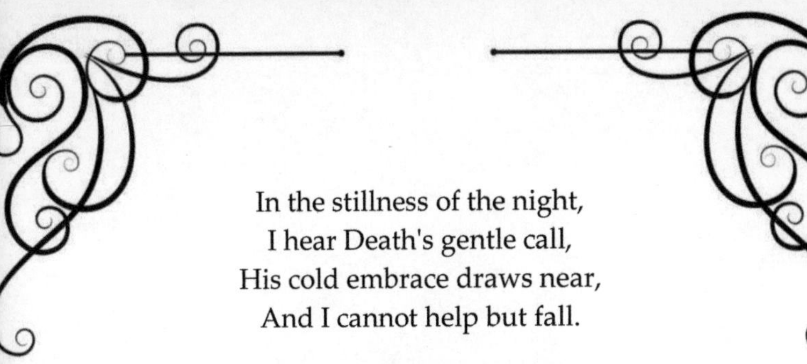

In the stillness of the night,
I hear Death's gentle call,
His cold embrace draws near,
And I cannot help but fall.

The darkness of his cloak,
Envelops me in its embrace,
And I feel his icy touch,
As he leads me to my place.

No more pain, no more sorrow,
No more tears to shed,
In Death's cold and silent realm,
I will rest my weary head.

But as I close my eyes,
And bid the world goodbye,
I wonder what awaits me,
In Death's eternal sky.

Will I find peace and solace,
Or eternal torment and pain,
As I enter Death's realm,
Will I ever see the light again?

But for now I rest in Death's embrace,
As the world fades away,
And in his cold and loving arms,
I surrender to my fate.

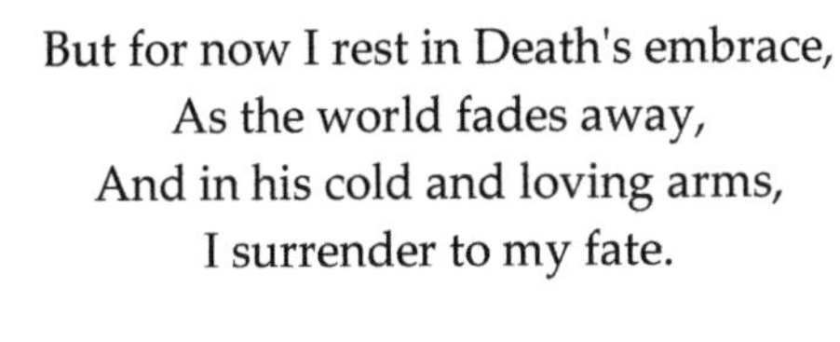

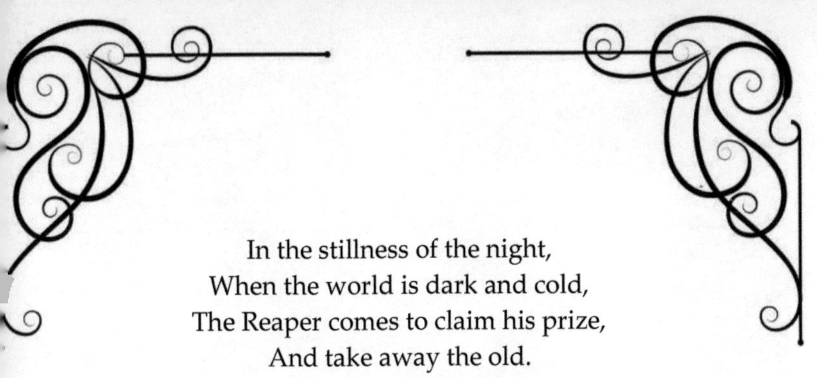

In the stillness of the night,
When the world is dark and cold,
The Reaper comes to claim his prize,
And take away the old.

He whispers in their ears,
And they feel his icy breath,
As he takes their hand and leads them,
To the realm of endless death.

No tears can stop his march,
No prayers can hold him back,
For he is the lord of the underworld,
And he rules with an iron knack.

He takes the young and old alike,
Without a moment's pause,
And leaves behind a grieving world,
To mourn and weep and pause.

So when you hear his call,
And feel his bony hand,
Remember that it's just the end,
Of a journey that we all must stand.

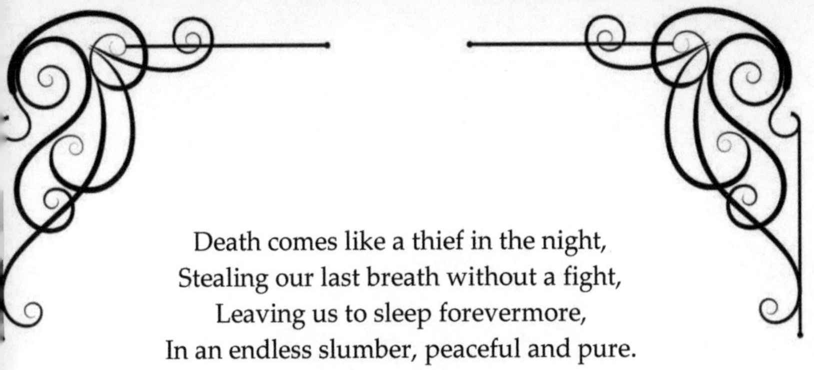

Death comes like a thief in the night,
Stealing our last breath without a fight,
Leaving us to sleep forevermore,
In an endless slumber, peaceful and pure.

The body grows cold, the eyes grow dim,
As the soul departs, leaving only skin,
And those left behind, with tears in their eyes,
Mourn for the ones who've left this life.

But is death the end, or is there more?
A place beyond this earthly shore,
Where souls may wander, free from pain,
In a world where death is but a gain.

Perhaps death is not the end,
But the beginning of a journey, my friend,
A passage to a new world, bright and fair,
Where loved ones await, beyond our earthly care.

So do not fear the end that comes to all,
But embrace it, as the final call,
To a place where pain and sorrow cease,
And we may rest in eternal peace.

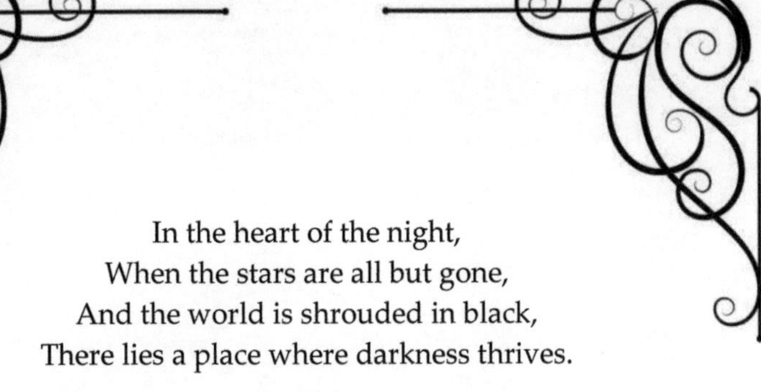

In the heart of the night,
When the stars are all but gone,
And the world is shrouded in black,
There lies a place where darkness thrives.

It's a place where nightmares are born,
And the shadows come to life,
Where every sound is a whisper of fear,
And every movement a portent of doom.

In the darkness, there is no hope,
No light to guide the way,
Only the cold embrace of emptiness,
And the endless expanse of the void.

But even in the depths of the night,
There is a glimmer of hope,
For in the darkest of places,
We can find the strength to persevere.

So let the darkness wash over you,
And embrace the fear within,
For it is only through facing our fears,
That we can ever hope to win.

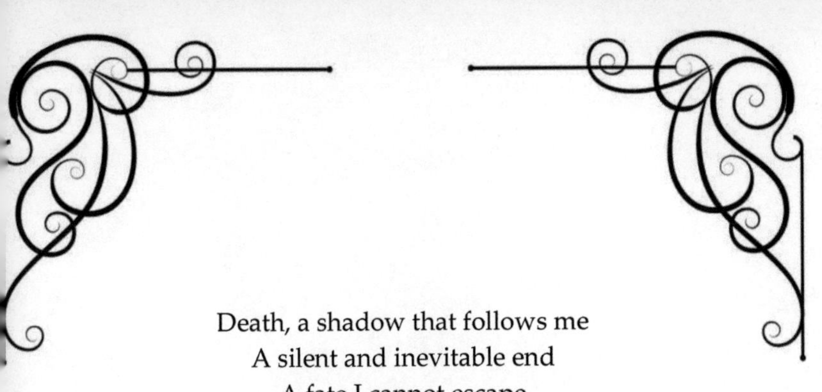

Death, a shadow that follows me
A silent and inevitable end
A fate I cannot escape
No matter how I bend

It creeps up slowly, day by day
A reminder of my mortality
A weight that I cannot shake
A burden to my reality

I try to run and hide away
But it always catches up
A specter that I cannot evade
A presence that will not let up

So I face it with a heavy heart
And accept my fate with grace
For in the end, we all depart
To a final resting place

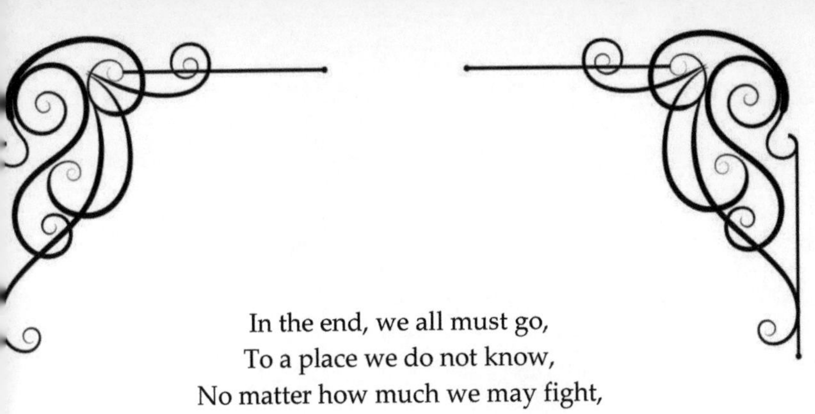

In the end, we all must go,
To a place we do not know,
No matter how much we may fight,
Death comes for us, day or night.

Some say it's just a part of life,
A natural end to all our strife,
But for those left behind to mourn,
It's a pain that cannot be borne.

We try to hold on to memories,
Of those who've left this mortal disease,
But time will pass, and memories fade,
Until all that's left is the pain we've made.

Yet even in the depths of despair,
We must remember those who were there,
And know that though they may be gone,
Their spirit lives on and on.

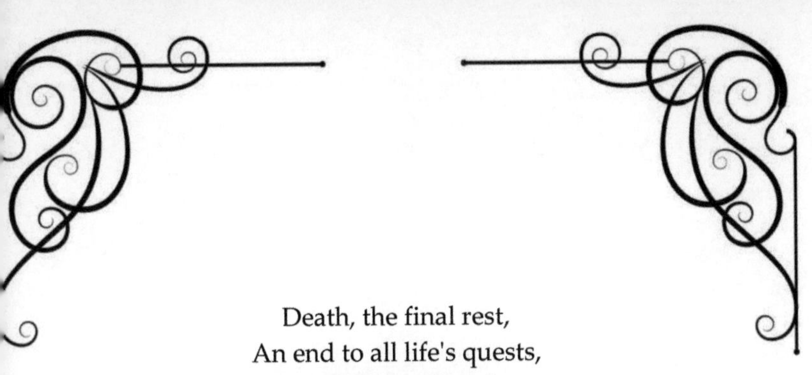

Death, the final rest,
An end to all life's quests,
A peaceful slumber deep,
In eternal sleep.

No more worries or fears,
No more pain or tears,
Just silence and release,
In eternal peace.

The cycle of life complete,
No more battles to defeat,
The soul finally at ease,
In eternal release.

And though we mourn the loss,
And feel the heavy cost,
We must remember to keep,
The memory of eternal sleep.

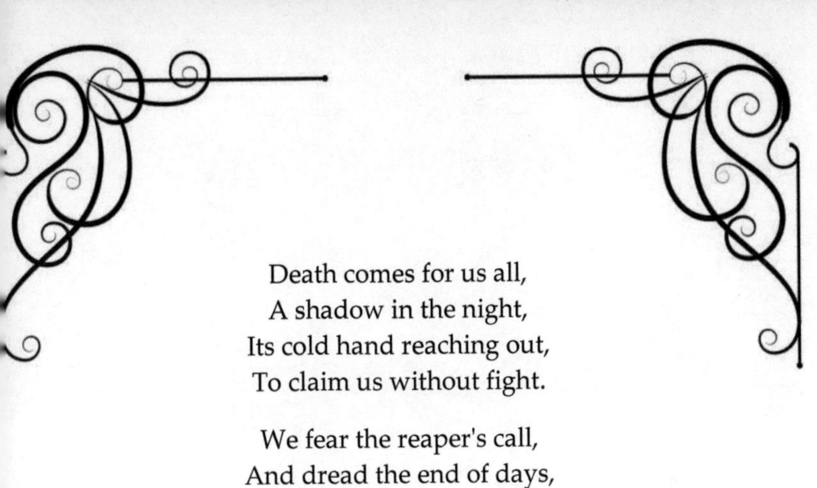

Death comes for us all,
A shadow in the night,
Its cold hand reaching out,
To claim us without fight.

We fear the reaper's call,
And dread the end of days,
For in its grasp we know,
Our mortal form decays.

But death is not the end,
For some believe it so,
And in the afterlife,
Our souls will surely go.

So though we fear the reaper,
And the unknown beyond the veil,
We must accept our fate,
And let death's wind fill our sail.

For life is but a fleeting moment,
In the grand scheme of things,
And in death we find release,
And the peace that it brings.

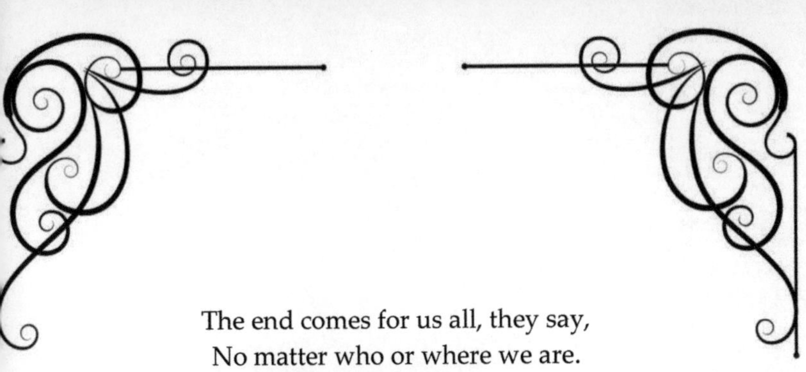

The end comes for us all, they say,
No matter who or where we are.
It lingers on the horizon,
Like a silent, looming star.

We try to hide from its shadow,
And ignore its icy grip,
But in the end, it claims us all,
And our souls begin to slip.

Some meet it with a smile,
And some with bitter tears,
But all must face the final act,
As the curtain slowly nears.

And though we cannot cheat death,
We can make our lives worth living,
And leave behind a legacy,
That will keep our memory living.

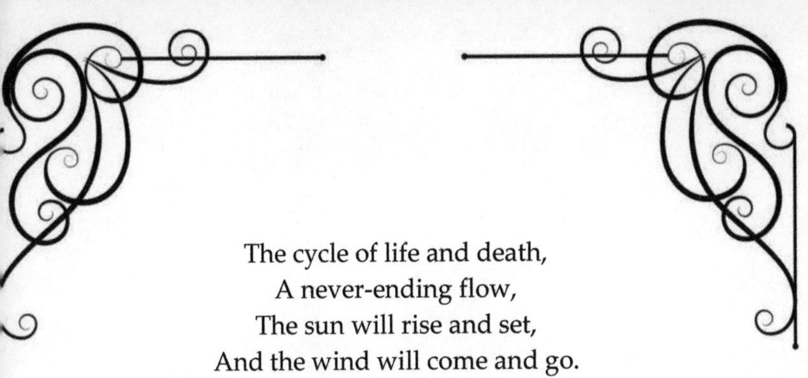

The cycle of life and death,
A never-ending flow,
The sun will rise and set,
And the wind will come and go.

The leaves will turn to brown,
And fall upon the ground,
The flowers will wilt away,
And new ones will be found.

The animals will come and go,
Their lives a fleeting spark,
And though they'll fade away,
Their memory will leave a mark.

And so we live our lives,
A momentary flame,
And though we'll all be gone someday,
Our legacy remains.

For life is but a cycle,
A never-ending wheel,
And though we may not understand,
It's beauty we can feel.

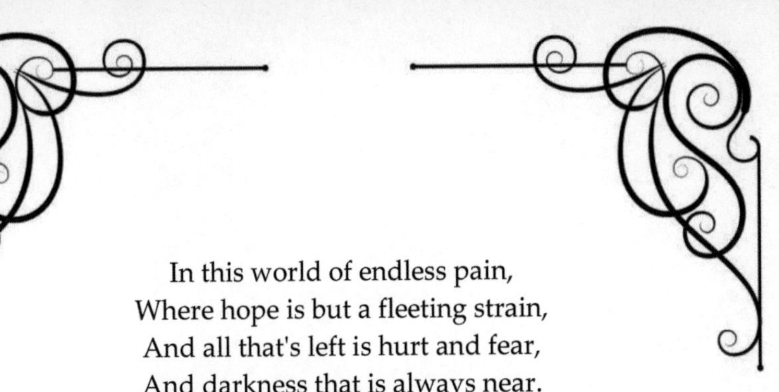

In this world of endless pain,
Where hope is but a fleeting strain,
And all that's left is hurt and fear,
And darkness that is always near.

The skies above are always gray,
The sun has long since gone away,
And all we see is endless night,
And all we feel is endless blight.

The love we had has turned to dust,
Our dreams are shattered, lost and rust,
And all that's left is emptiness,
A void that we can never bless.

The future's bleak, the past is gone,
The present's but a bitter dawn,
And all we have is pain and sorrow,
That we will carry to tomorrow.

So let us weep, let us mourn,
For all the joys that we have shorn,
And let us pray for sweet release,
And hope for an eternal peace.

In this empty room, I sit alone
My thoughts are all I have to call my own
The silence is deafening, and so is the pain
As I try to forget, but the memories remain

The walls seem to close in, as I suffocate
In this lonely abyss, where nothing is great
The shadows dance around, mocking my plight
As I struggle to find, a glimmer of light

The emptiness consumes me,
and I can't escape
The darkness that surrounds me,
and the fear that's so great
I'm lost in this maze, with no way out
As I try to scream, but no sound comes out

The tears fall like rain, as I cry out in pain
In this emptiness, I have nothing to gain
I'm just a shell of who I used to be
Lost in this void, with no one to see

So I sit in this room, and let the silence take over
As I try to forget, but it's all I remember
The emptiness is my home,
and the darkness my friend
As I wait for the end, with nothing left to mend.

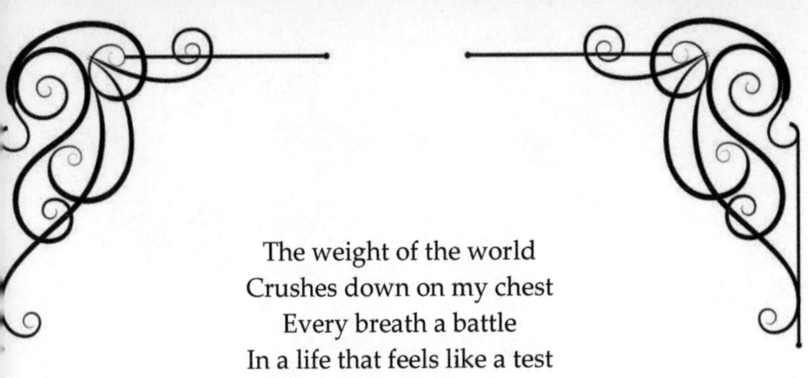

The weight of the world
Crushes down on my chest
Every breath a battle
In a life that feels like a test

The darkness surrounds me
And I can't find my way
The future feels hopeless
And the past won't go away

My heart is heavy
With sadness and despair
And the thought of tomorrow
Feels too much to bear

I try to find a glimmer
Of hope or light
But it's all just darkness
In this never-ending night

The tears won't stop falling
And the pain won't go away
In this life that's so hard
And grows darker each day.

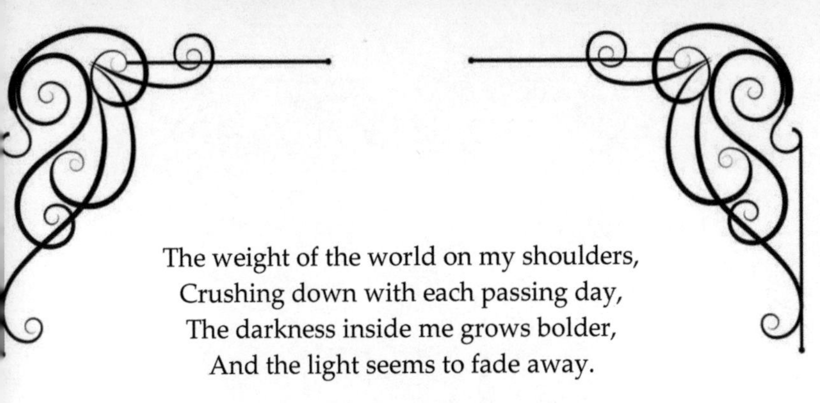

The weight of the world on my shoulders,
Crushing down with each passing day,
The darkness inside me grows bolder,
And the light seems to fade away.

I try to find hope in the little things,
But they slip through my fingers like sand,
The future feels like an endless sting,
And I can't escape the grip of this hand.

The world keeps turning, but I stand still,
A prisoner to my own despair,
The void inside me only seems to fill,
And the pain is too much to bear.

I long for an end to this endless plight,
A release from this never-ending sorrow,
But all I see is the eternal night,
And the hope for a better tomorrow is hollow.

So I sit in the darkness, alone and still,
With nothing but my thoughts to keep me company,
And I wonder if this is my destiny, my will,
To be forever lost in this misery.

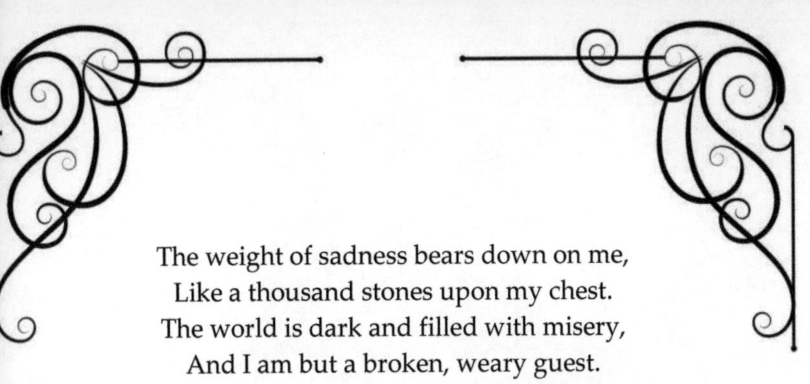

The weight of sadness bears down on me,
Like a thousand stones upon my chest.
The world is dark and filled with misery,
And I am but a broken, weary guest.

I search for light amidst the gloom,
But all I find are shadows and despair.
My heart is heavy, filled with doom,
And I can't escape this life of care.

The tears I shed are like a river,
Flowing endlessly down my face.
My soul is battered, torn asunder,
And I can't escape this cruel, dark place.

I long for peace, for sweet release,
From the torment of my mind.
But all I feel is endless grief,
And no relief can I find.

So I will wander through this life,
A lost and broken soul.
Until at last the final strife,
And death will claim its toll.

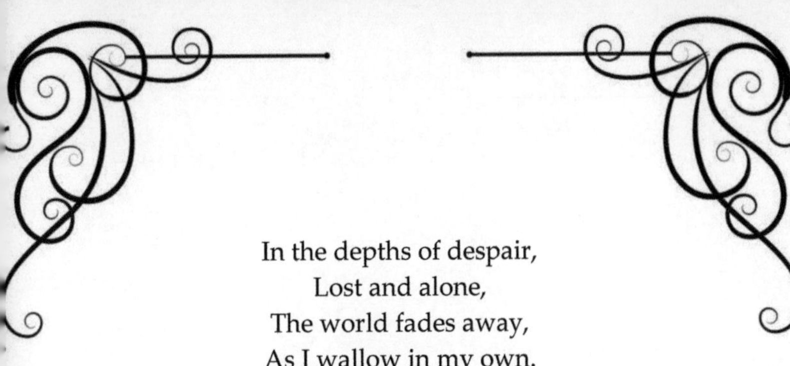

In the depths of despair,
Lost and alone,
The world fades away,
As I wallow in my own.

The darkness consumes,
All that I hold dear,
Leaving nothing but emptiness,
And crushing me with fear.

Each breath is a struggle,
As I try to hold on,
But the weight of my sorrow,
Is just too strong.

The tears flow like rivers,
As I cry out in pain,
Hoping for a glimmer of hope,
But it never comes again.

And so I sit here,
In the silence of the night,
Lost and alone,
With no end in sight.

A hollow existence, a life full of pain,
Every day is a struggle, a constant refrain,
The weight on my shoulders, too heavy to bear,
My heart is in pieces, my soul stripped bare.

The world is so dark, so cold and so bleak,
I'm lost in the darkness, unable to speak,
My tears fall like rain, a never-ending stream,
As I cling to the hope of a shattered dream.

I'm drowning in sorrow, consumed by despair,
No one can see me, no one seems to care,
My cries go unheard, my voice is so small,
I'm fading away, I'm losing it all.

The days stretch on endlessly, a never-ending pain,
I'm trapped in this cycle, again and again,
There's no escape from the demons within,
I'm lost in this darkness, with no way to win.

A hollow existence, a life full of pain,
Every day is a struggle, a constant refrain,
But I'll keep on fighting, I won't give in,
For one day I'll find the light,
and my soul will begin to mend.

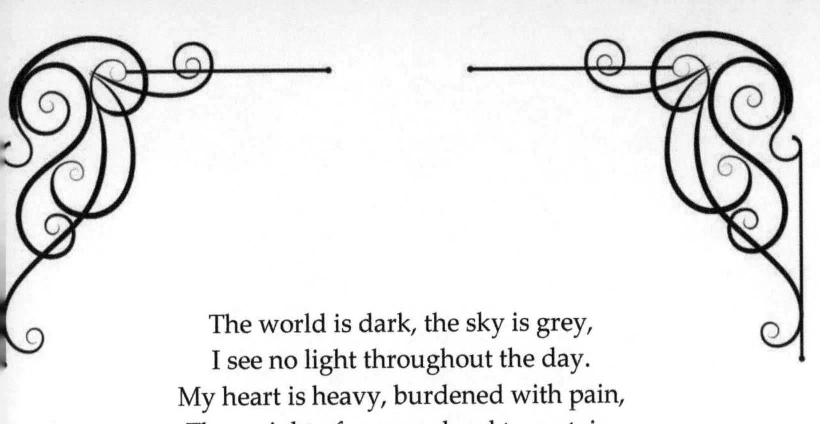

The world is dark, the sky is grey,
I see no light throughout the day.
My heart is heavy, burdened with pain,
The weight of sorrow, hard to sustain.

The world moves on, indifferent and cold,
As I struggle with this heavy load.
I try to smile, to fake some cheer,
But the emptiness inside is clear.

I long for peace, for release from this pain,
But it seems that hope is all in vain.
So I trudge along, day after day,
In this dark and dismal way.

Perhaps one day, the light will shine,
And I'll feel something more than just decline.
Until then, I'll keep my head low,
And bear the weight of this endless woe.

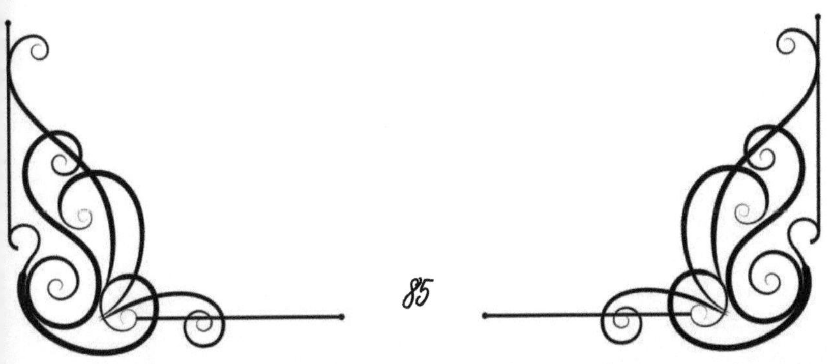

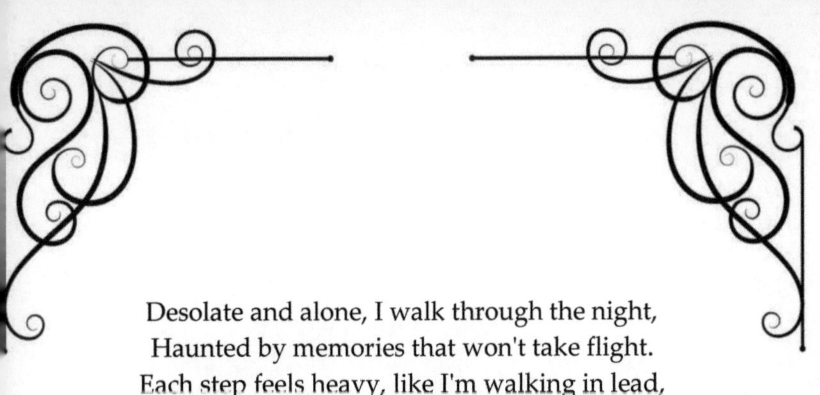

Desolate and alone, I walk through the night,
Haunted by memories that won't take flight.
Each step feels heavy, like I'm walking in lead,
And the darkness around me, fills me with dread.

The weight of my sorrows, I carry with care,
As I wander aimlessly, with nowhere to spare.
All the joy that I knew, has long since fled,
And my soul feels barren, like I'm already dead.

The stars up above, seem so far away,
As if they're mocking me, for the price I must pay.
I'm left with nothing, but a hollow inside,
As I search for meaning, but find none to abide.

My heart is aching, and my spirit is low,
I'm consumed by sadness, and I can't let it go.
I pray for redemption, but it's too late for me,
For death is the only escape, from this misery.

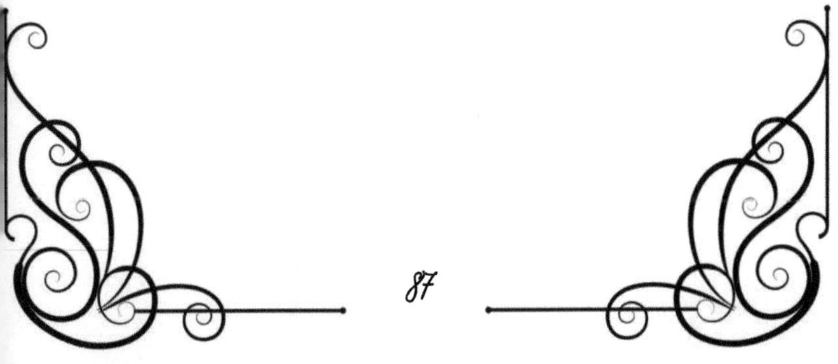

In the silence of the night,
I feel the darkness creeping in,
And all the things I've left behind,
Come crawling back again.

The memories of my past mistakes,
The regrets that I can't shake,
They haunt me with their ghostly wails,
And never give me a break.

I try to run and hide away,
But they always find me in the end,
And every time I close my eyes,
I see the darkness descend.

It's like a weight upon my soul,
That I can never shed,
And every breath that I take,
Feels like I'm already dead.

So I sit here in the darkness,
And I let the tears run free,
As I wait for the final blow,
To set me free from me.

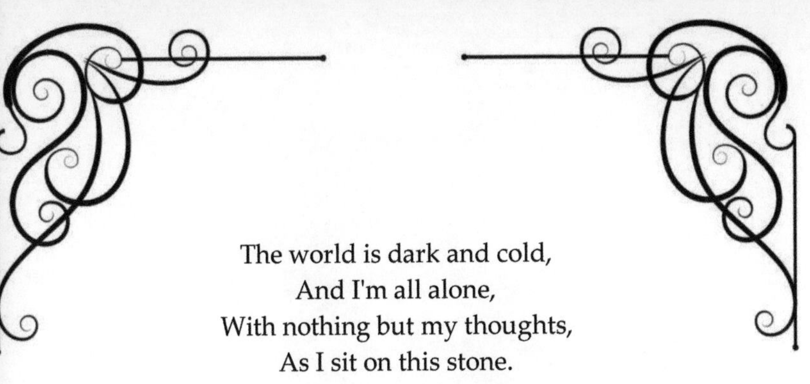

The world is dark and cold,
And I'm all alone,
With nothing but my thoughts,
As I sit on this stone.

The memories of the past,
Are all that I have left,
And every moment that goes by,
Leaves me more bereft.

I've lost so much in this life,
And gained so little in return,
And now I'm just a shell,
With nothing left to burn.

The emptiness consumes me,
As I stare into the abyss,
And I wonder if it's worth it,
To continue on like this.

But I'll keep on moving forward,
For there's nothing left to do,
And maybe someday in the future,
I'll find some purpose anew.

The darkness falls and I am alone,
With nothing but my thoughts to keep me company.
I sit and stare into the void,
Wondering what lies beyond.

The weight of my sorrows drags me down,
And I feel as though I'll never escape.
I search for hope but find only despair,
And wonder if anyone truly cares.

The night grows deeper and the stars shine bright,
But I cannot find solace in their light.
I am lost in a sea of my own pain,
And fear that I will never rise again.

But still I cling to the hope that one day,
The darkness will lift and the sun will shine.
And though it may be hard to believe,
I know that somehow, I will survive.

In shattered pieces on the ground,
Lie dreams that once were found,
The hope that filled our hearts and minds,
Has left us all behind.

The future once so bright and clear,
Is now consumed by fear,
The paths we thought we'd take in life,
Have vanished in the strife.

And though we try to mend the pieces,
The pain just never eases,
For what was once a beautiful dream,
Has now become a hopeless scheme.

So we try to move on day by day,
In hopes that we may find a way,
To heal the wounds and ease the pain,
And start anew once again.

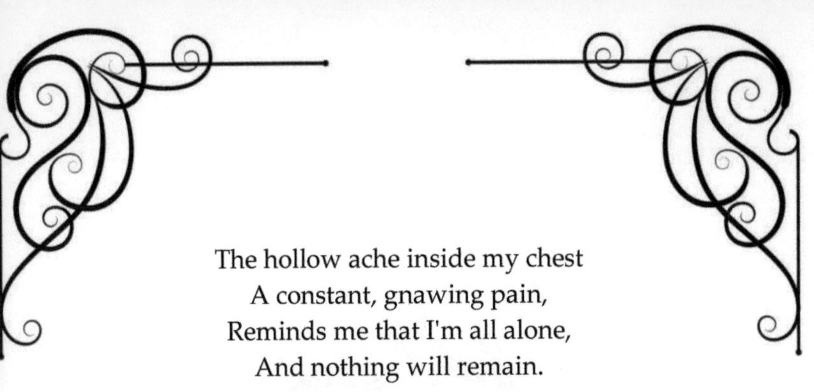

The hollow ache inside my chest
A constant, gnawing pain,
Reminds me that I'm all alone,
And nothing will remain.

The memories that once were dear,
Now haunt me like a curse,
A reminder of the love I've lost,
And how it could've been worse.

I wander through this empty world,
A shadow of my past,
And though I try to move ahead,
I can't escape the last.

The emptiness consumes me whole,
And leaves me feeling numb,
A life without a purpose,
A future that's undone.

So I sit and wait for something,
Anything to change my fate,
But nothing ever comes along,
And I remain, empty, in this state.

Eine Welt voller Bücher

Unvergessliche Abenteuer
Faszinierende Charaktere
Neue Welten und Ideen

Bei Infinity Gaze endet
die Lesereise nie!

Jetzt entdecken unter:
www.infinitygaze.com